**This
Christmas Cracker
belongs to:**

_____

_____

First published 1989 by Walker Books Ltd
87 Vauxhall Walk, London SE11 5HJ
This edition published 2010
2 4 6 8 10 9 7 5 3 1
Illustrations © 1989 Lis Toft
The right of Lis Toft to be identified as illustrator of this work has been asserted by her
in accordance with the Copyright, Designs and Patents Act 1988
Printed in China
British Library Cataloguing in Publication Data:
a catalogue record for this book is available from the British Library
978-1-4063-3314-5
www.walker.co.uk

The Night Before
Christmas

Written by
Clement C. Moore

Illustrated by
Lis Toft

WALKER BOOKS
AND SUBSIDIARIES
LONDON • BOSTON • SYDNEY • AUCKLAND

'Twas the night before Christmas, when
   all through the house
Not a creature was stirring, not even
   a mouse;
The stockings were hung by
   the chimney with care,
In hope that St. Nicholas soon
   would be there;

The children were nestled all snug in their beds
While visions of sugar plums danced in their
  heads;
And Mama in her kerchief, and I in my cap,
Had just settled our brains for a long
  winter's nap,

When out on the lawn there arose such a clatter,
I sprang from my bed to see what was the matter.
Away to the window I flew like a flash,
Tore open the shutters and threw up the sash.

The moon on the breast of the new-fallen snow
Gave a lustre of midday to objects below,
When, what to my wondering eyes should
  appear,
But a miniature sleigh and eight tiny reindeer,
With a little old driver, so lively and quick,
I knew in a moment it must be St. Nick.

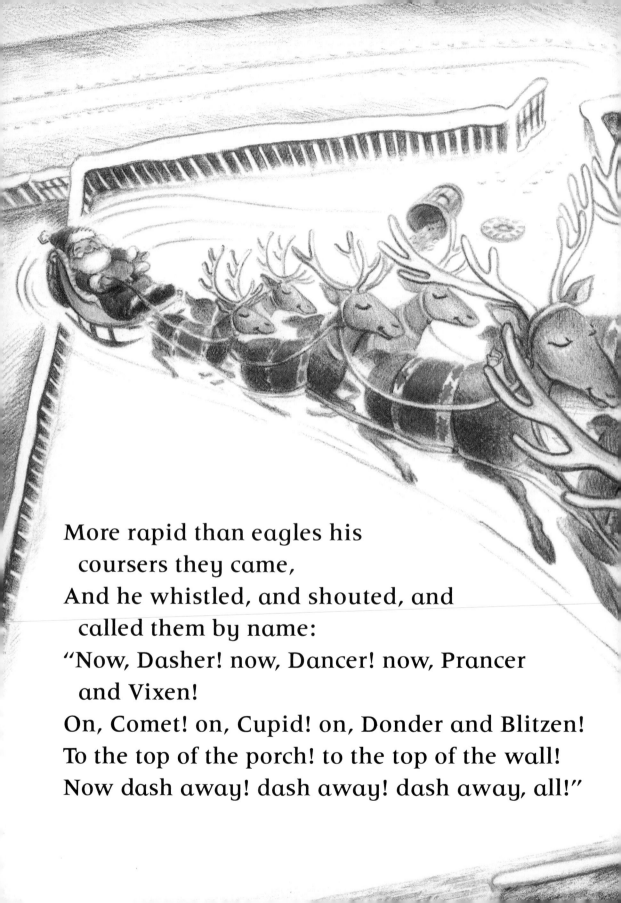

More rapid than eagles his
  coursers they came,
And he whistled, and shouted, and
  called them by name:
"Now, Dasher! now, Dancer! now, Prancer
  and Vixen!
On, Comet! on, Cupid! on, Donder and Blitzen!
To the top of the porch! to the top of the wall!
Now dash away! dash away! dash away, all!"

As dry leaves that before the wild hurricane fly,
When they meet with an obstacle, mount to
  the sky,
So up to the house-top the coursers
  they flew,
With a sleigh full of toys, and St.
  Nicholas, too.

And then, in a twinkling, I heard on the roof
The prancing and pawing of each little hoof.
As I drew in my head, and was turning
  around,
Down the chimney St. Nicholas came
  with a bound.

He was dressed all
  in fur, from his head to his foot,
And his clothes were all tarnished with ashes
  and soot;
A bundle of toys he had flung on his back,
and he looked like a pedlar just opening
  his pack.
His eyes – how they twinkled! his dimples,
  how merry!
His cheeks were like roses, his nose like a cherry!

His droll little mouth was drawn up like a bow,
And the beard on his chin was as white as
  the snow;
The stump of his pipe he held tight in his teeth,
And the smoke, it encircled his head like
  a wreath;
He had a broad face and a little round belly
That shook, when he laughed, like a bowl
  full of jelly.

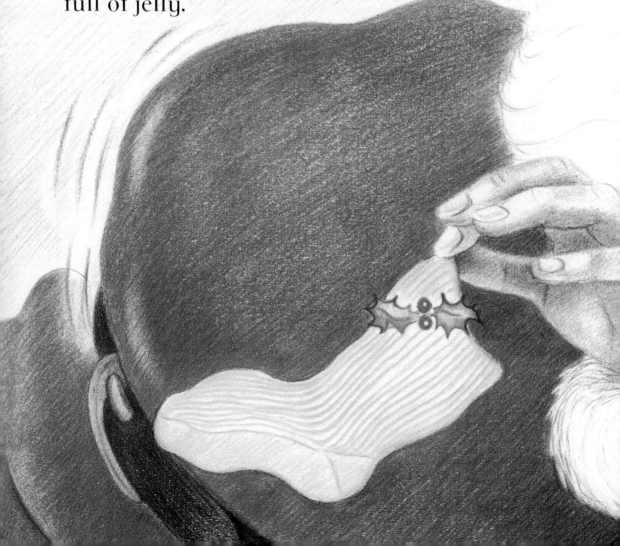

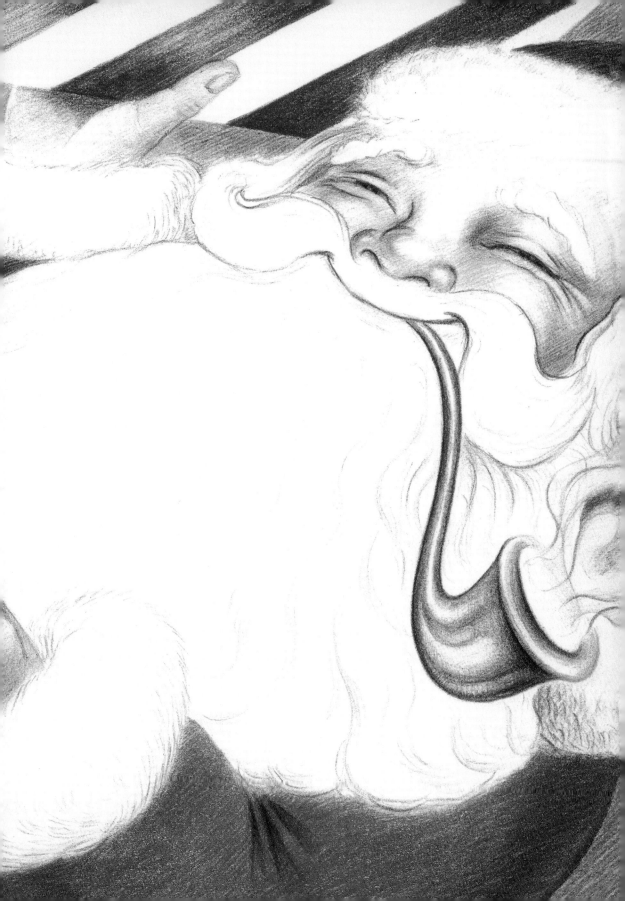

He was chubby and plump, a right jolly old elf,
And I laughed when I saw him, in spite
  of myself;
A wink of his eye and a twist of his head,
Soon gave me to know I had nothing to dread;
He spoke not a word, but went straight to
  his work,
And filled all the stockinys; then turned with
  a jerk,

And laying a finger aside of his nose,
And giving a nod, up the chimney he rose.

He sprang to his sleigh, to his team gave
  a whistle,
And away they all flew like the down of
  a thistle.
But I heard him exclaim, ere he drove out
  of sight,
"Happy Christmas to all,
And to all a good night!"